W9-BNQ-915

Girls Play to Win

SOFTBALL

by Marty Gitlin

Content Consultant
Karen Johns
Coach and Former Player
USA Softball

NORWOOD HOUSE PRESS
CHICAGO, ILLINOIS

Norwood House Press
P.O. Box 316598
Chicago, Illinois 60631

For information regarding Norwood House Press, please visit our website at
www.norwoodhousepress.com or call 866-565-2900.

Photo Credits: Leonardo Ramirez/AP Images, cover, 1; Amy Sancetta/AP Images, 4,
50; Bigstock, 6, 11, 14, 16, 18, 19, 37, 39; Red Line Editorial, 12; X.O. Howe/Library of
Congress, 20; Herbert A. French/Library of Congress, 23; Library of Congress, 27, 33;
AP Images, 28; FAU Athletic Media Relations, 34; UCLA Sports Information, 41; Eric
Draper/AP Images, 42; Joe Cavaretta/AP Images, 46; Ng Han Guan/AP Images, 49;
Fernando Liano/AP Images, 53; Alonzo Adams/AP Images, 57; Marty Gitlin, 64 (top);
ASA/USA Softball, 64 (bottom)

Editor: Chrös McDougall
Series Design: Christa Schneider
Project Management: Red Line Editorial

Library of Congress Cataloging-in-Publication Data

Gitlin, Marty.
Girls play to win softball / by Marty Gitlin.
  p. cm. -- (Girls play to win)
Includes bibliographical references and index.
 Summary: "Covers the history, rules, fundamentals, and significant
personalities of the sport of women's softball. Topics include: techniques,
strategies, competitive events, and equipment. Glossary, Additional
Resources, and Index included"--Provided by publisher.
ISBN-13: 978-1-59953-465-7 (library edition : alk. paper)
ISBN-10: 1-59953-465-7 (library edition : alk. paper)
1. Softball for women--Juvenile literature. 2. Softball for
children--Juvenile literature. I. Title.
GV881.3.G58 2011
796.357'8082--dc22

                           2011011051

Manufactured in the United States of America in North Mankato, Minnesota.
198R—032012

Girls Play to Win
SOFTBALL

Table of Contents

CHAPTER 1 Softball Basics 4

CHAPTER 2 Strange Start to Softball 20

CHAPTER 3 A Growing Game 28

CHAPTER 4 Breaking Through 34

CHAPTER 5 Going Global 42

CHAPTER 6 Playing to Win 50

Glossary 58
For More Information 60
Index 62
Places to Visit 64
About the Author and Content Consultant 64

Words in **bold type** are defined in the glossary.

▲ Team USA's Cat Osterman hurls
a pitch during the 2008 Olympic Games.

CHAPTER 1

SOFTBALL
BASICS

When it comes to dominating a sport, few can match Cat Osterman. She is one of the finest fast-pitch softball players in the world. While at the University of Texas, she was named USA Softball Collegiate Player of the Year three times. She pitched 14.2 **shutout innings** in leading the United States to a gold medal in the 2004 Olympic Games. She pitched 17 more to help Team USA to a silver medal four years later. Osterman has also starred in the National Pro Fastpitch (NPF) **professional** league. And she twice graced the cover of *Sports Illustrated* magazine.

So how did Osterman achieve those great feats? She credits her success to hard work. "I guess that's how I was brought up," she said. "My parents and I work hard for everything we have. My dad never forced me into softball at all. But he said that if I was going to play softball, I should give it everything I had. And that's what I've done."

Indeed, Osterman has achieved incredible success. But she is only one of millions of young women who have embraced the sport. Today, softball is among the most popular girls' sports in the United States.

GETTING STARTED

The two basic forms of softball are slow-pitch and fast-pitch. These days, nearly all youth, high school, college, and elite-level softball is fast-pitch. Slow-pitch softball is primarily played casually or for recreation. The slow-pitch games are basically the same but with a few minor rule changes.

Softball was developed as a form of baseball, so it is no surprise that the sports share many similarities. Each softball team has nine players who are active at a given time. Each game lasts seven innings. Whichever team scores more **runs** during those innings wins. If the score

▲ *A batter hits the ball toward the third baseman.*

is tied after seven innings, the teams continue to play **extra innings** until one team has a higher score than the other at the end of a full inning.

Each inning is divided into two halves. During the first half of each inning, the home team plays in the field, or on defense, while the away team bats. Once the fielding team records three outs, the teams switch. Now the home team bats while the away team is in the field. Once the away team records three outs, the inning is over.

All nine active players on a softball team are given a defensive position and a batting position. The defensive position determines the area of the field in which the player is located while playing defense. The batting position is her place in the batting order. Players can switch defensive positions during a game, but they cannot switch places in the batting order. In addition, each team also has players who start the game on the bench as substitutes. They can replace one of the nine players in both the field and the batting order during a game.

PITCHER V. BATTER

The main battle in softball is between the pitcher and batter. The pitcher is on the defensive team. She begins each play by hurling the ball underhand toward the catcher, who is waiting behind **home plate**. The batter stands next

Softball v. Baseball

There are a few primary differences between softball and baseball. Perhaps the most noticeable difference is that softball pitchers throw the ball underhand while baseball pitchers throw it overhand. One benefit to throwing underhand is that it causes less arm strain for the pitcher, allowing her to stay in games longer and to play more frequently. Another major difference between the sports is the size of the field. For example, in softball, the distance between home plate and the **pitching rubber** is 43 feet (13.1 m) compared to 60 feet, 6 inches (18.4 m) in baseball. Additionally, softball bases are 60 feet (18.3 m) apart while baseball bases are 90 feet (27.4 m) apart. The third major difference is the size of the balls. Softballs have a 12-inch (30.5-cm) circumference while baseballs have a nine-inch (22.9 cm) circumference.

to home plate. Her goal is to get on base either by hitting the ball into play or getting a **walk**. The pitcher's goal is to get the batter out.

An **umpire** is positioned behind the catcher. Among his or her duties is to determine the **strike zone** for each batter. The strike zone is an invisible square that is the width of home plate and runs approximately from the batter's knees to her shoulders. The umpire calls any pitch thrown through that zone a **strike**. Strikes are considered hittable balls. A batter can also get a strike by swinging and missing at a pitch or hitting a **foul** ball, which is a hit ball that lands outside the field of play. A strikeout occurs if the pitcher records three strikes in one **at-bat**.

Another result that can occur is a base on balls, which is commonly referred to as a walk. That occurs if the pitcher throws four **balls** during an at-bat. If the batter is walked, she automatically advances to first base. If a teammate is already on first base, the teammate advances as well. If the bases are loaded when a player is walked, the player on third base advances to home plate and scores a run.

The third possible result of an at-bat is that the batter hits the ball into play. A player who safely reaches base has accomplished a **hit**. However, the team on defense can still record an out on a ball hit into play. The easiest way to do that is by catching the ball before it hits the ground. That results in an automatic out.

The defense can also register an out if the ball is hit on the ground. One way to do that is by a **force** play. A force play occurs when the base runner has no choice but to advance to the next base. Any time a batter hits the ball into play there is a force play at first base because she must run to that base. Similarly, if a runner starts a play on first base, she must run to second base on a ball hit into play. That means there is a force play at first and second base.

To record an out on a force play, a defensive player must gain possession of the ball and touch the base in question before the runner. This often involves an infielder fielding the ball and throwing it to the first baseman.

Catch That Ball!

Fielding is one of the most important skills in softball. To field a ground ball, move quickly toward the ball and get in front of it. Don't be afraid of it or shy away if it is traveling fast. Open the glove to field the ball and make sure it is secure. The key to catching fly balls is to take the shortest distance to the ball. Run fast toward the ball so you are planted and ready to catch it. Open the glove and watch as the ball soars into it. It is also important to use your free hand to secure the ball so that it doesn't pop out of your glove after catching it.

Making the Throw

Before you throw the ball, make sure you are gripping it securely. Hold the ball in your fingers, not your palm. Place the thumb on the opposite side for a strong grip. But don't hold the ball too tightly. Keep the foot on the other side of your throwing arm back and pointed to the target. So if you throw with your right hand, your left foot should be pointed forward and vice versa. Stride forward with that other foot as you draw your throwing arm back. Rotate your hips and upper body while firing the ball. Don't push the ball forward. Follow your arm through to the target. Practice these steps until they become a habit.

If there is not a force play, a defensive player can still record an out by tagging the base runner. As long as the base runner is not touching a base, she is vulnerable to being tagged out.

GET A HIT, SCORE A RUN

The goal of the batting team is to score as many runs as possible. A run is scored when a player safely advances to first base, then to second base, then to third base, and then to home plate. The easiest way to do that is by hitting a **home run**. A home run is a ball that is hit in the air over the outfield fence. A batter who does that automatically gets to run around the bases and score a run. Any teammates who were already on base get to score as well.

▲ *The first baseman catches the ball just before the runner touches first base to record an out.*

Home runs are rare. They require a powerful swing that hits the ball just right. Even then, getting the ball over the outfield fence isn't guaranteed. Because of that, most runs are scored as part of a **rally**. A rally is when the batting team combines a series of hits and walks to score runs.

In softball, each defensive position is assigned a number, as shown in the diagram at right. They are pitcher (1), catcher (2), first baseman (3), second baseman (4), third baseman (5), shortstop (6), left fielder (7), center fielder (8), and right fielder (9). Those numbers are used in scoring. For example, a fly ball caught by the left fielder would be scored: F-7. A ground ball hit to the shortstop, who then throws the runner out at first would be recorded: 6-3.

If the batter drives the ball into play and reaches first base before the defense can get the ball to first base, then she has recorded a hit. In softball, a batter who safely reaches first base on one hit has gotten a single. If she reaches second base she has hit a double. If she reaches third base she has hit a triple. Should the batter run all the way around the bases and safely touch home plate without hitting the ball over the outfield fence, she has hit an inside-the-park home run.

DEFENSIVE POSITIONS

Each of the nine players has a different position on the field when on defense. Their goal is to make outs. Each player is positioned in a place to best maximize her chances to do that.

The pitcher is the most important player on the field. She must have good balance on the mound. She also

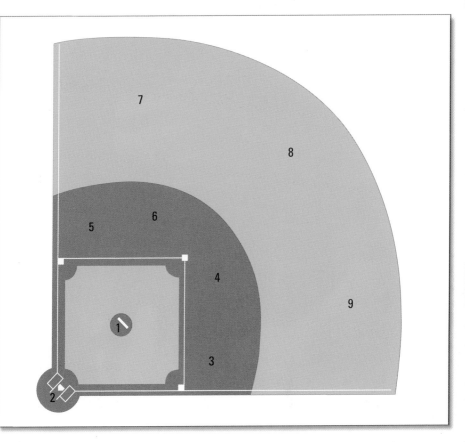

▲ *This diagram shows a softball field and the general area in which each position, listed by number, stands while on defense.*

requires the talent to prevent the batter from hitting the ball. That is achieved by either firing the ball with great speed or with a lot of movement. Many accomplished pitchers are able to throw balls that rise or drop. They do this by releasing the ball so that it is spinning in different directions. A ball that moves while flying toward the plate is much harder to hit than one moving in a straight line. A rise ball, for example, might look like it's coming in right at waist level before suddenly rising above the strike zone

▲ Catchers like this one wear extra equipment to protect themselves from foul tips and wild pitches.

at the last moment. Being able to pitch at varying speeds also helps keep a batter off balance. If a pitcher can throw some pitches fast and some much slower, it is harder for the batter to prepare for what is coming.

The catcher is also an important fielder. Her first duty is to make certain she catches the pitches cleanly. Some catchers also work with the manager and the pitcher to "call" the game. That means she helps guide the pitcher through what kind of pitches should be thrown. The manager often signals what pitch to throw to the catcher, who then signals it to the pitcher. For example, if a batter generally struggles hitting rise balls, the pitching team might call that the pitcher throw those pitches more often.

The left side of the infield consists of the third baseman and shortstop. The right side has the second baseman and first baseman. It is important for all four players to be quick and to have sure hands. They must be able to rush far to the left or right to catch ground balls. The shortstop and third baseman require strong throwing arms. They must often field ground balls and throw the ball quickly and accurately to the first baseman to record outs.

The left fielder, center fielder, and right fielder occupy the outfield positions. All should be quick to track down balls hit far from them. Their goal is to catch the balls and record an out. However, if an outfielder cannot catch the ball, her next goal is to make sure it does not get past

A batter makes contact with a pitch.

SLUGGING THAT SOFTBALL

Elite softball pitchers fire the ball up to 70 miles per hour (112.65 km/h) from usually only 43 feet (13.1 m) away. Hitting a softball takes great balance and hand-eye coordination. Good habits make good hitters. Bad habits cause slumps. The following suggestions were made by longtime college softball coach and author Dick "Smitty" Smith:

- *Follow the ball with your eyes from the pitcher's hand to the bat.*

- *Keep your hands back until you are ready to swing the bat. Don't let them drop. That will cause you to swing under the ball rather than hit it squarely.*

- *Take only a short stride with your front foot as you prepare to swing.*

- *Don't swing at bad pitches. Swing only at balls that should be called strikes and in your hitting zone.*

- *Practice, practice, practice!*

Confidence is important. If you follow Smith's advice you should be successful. And success breeds confidence.

her. If it lands or rolls behind the outfielder then the batter has more time to run to get on base and get extra bases. Outfielders also need to have strong arms so they can quickly throw active balls back into the infield to stop runners from advancing.

THE BATTING ORDER

While batting, or on offense, the nine players come up to bat one by one. The team decides which order the players bat before each game. The batting order is independent from the fielding positions. For example, the first baseman for one team might bat third, and the other team's first baseman could bat fifth.

The batting order is usually determined based on the strengths of each batter. The first batter is called the lead-off hitter. She is usually a fast runner and good at getting on base by either drawing walks or getting hits. Teams generally put their best hitters in the third and fourth spots. The theory is that the hitters who come up first and second can get on base and the strong hitters who come up third and fourth can drive them in to score runs.

Each team starts at the top of its batting order at the beginning of the game. After that, they begin each new inning where they left off the last one. So if a team uses five batters in the first inning before getting three outs, then the sixth batter leads off the next inning. After all nine batters have had an at-bat, the batting order starts

All defensive players use a glove.

BAT AND GLOVE

Most softball players basically only need a bat and glove. The bat should be the right length and weight for each player. A heavy bat will result in a slow swing. A bat that is too light will not provide enough power. Most bats are made out of aluminum or graphite/titanium. Batting helmets protect the head of the batter. Gloves differ slightly based on your position. For example, a catcher's glove has extra padding. An outfielder's glove is often longer, giving the player a bigger area in which to catch the ball. Catchers also wear more equipment than others. It includes a helmet, chest protector, and shin guards.

over from the top. The weakest hitters are usually at the bottom of the order so that the batters at the top of the order get more at-bats.

FAST OR SLOW?

Most competitive girls' and women's softball is fast-pitch. The primary difference between fast-pitch and slow-pitch is that fast-pitch pitchers use a windmill windup before throwing the ball. That gives their bodies momentum toward the plate and allows them to fire the ball as hard as possible. They also often try to make the ball rise or drop by spinning it.

Slow-pitch pitchers simply loft the ball toward home plate without the windmill windup. Each pitch has to arc a certain amount (depending on the league) to ensure that the pitcher is not throwing too

▲ *This softball team huddles so players can motivate each other before a big game.*

hard. These slower, arced pitches are much easier to hit. That often results in high-scoring games.

Because slow-pitch softball is often played for recreation, the rules sometimes differ depending on who is playing. There are some other general differences between the two styles, though. Slow-pitch softball teams often have 10 players on the field rather than the usual nine. The extra player is usually added to the outfield. Fast-pitch softball also allows base runners to **steal**. That means a player on base can attempt to run to the next base as soon as the pitcher lets go of the ball. This is not allowed in slow-pitch softball.

Regardless of which version you prefer, softball is always a fun game to play!

▲ *This "indoor base ball" team from Chicago, shown around 1887, is considered the first softball team.*

CHAPTER 2

STRANGE START TO SOFTBALL

On Thanksgiving Day in 1887, a group of approximately 20 men met at the Farragut Boat Club gymnasium in Chicago, Illinois. The men were eagerly waiting to hear the result of a college football game played that day. They had bets riding on the outcome of the annual clash between Harvard and Yale. And those who wagered on Yale celebrated when told their team had won.

One Yale fan showed his excitement. He picked up a boxing glove and tossed it underhand at a Harvard booster, who smacked it with a pole. The glove went flying.

Nobody gave this playful exchange much thought. Nobody, that is, but a reporter named George Hancock. He had a brainstorm. What he just saw greatly resembled baseball, which was already an established sport at the time. So he tied the strings around the boxing glove and grabbed a broomstick handle. He chalked out a **diamond** on the gym floor.

"Let's play ball!" he shouted.

And that's just what the men did. The men pitched, hit, caught, and threw that boxing glove until an incredible 80 runs were scored. Although their "indoor base ball" game looked very different from today's fast-pitch softball, it was considered the sport's first game.

It might have also been the last game had Hancock not seen a future in it. He gathered the men around and asked them to come back that Saturday. By that time he would have a new bat, new ball, and new rules. True to his word, he returned with an oversized ball and rubber-tipped bat. He had also painted a permanent diamond on the floor. That soft, oversized ball became the first softball.

The game they played was described in the following excerpt from the *Indoor Base Ball Guide*:

Running to Third

Some organizations came up with strange rules during the early days of softball. The National Amateur Playground Ball Association (NAPBA) of the United States was formed in 1908 (some people called the sport "Playground Ball" at the time). It created some of those rules. One rule allowed the first batter of every inning to run to third base instead of first after hitting the ball. She would score by reaching second base, first base, and then home. Another rule stated that games could be decided by a point total rather than runs scored. A point was awarded every time a runner reached base. These rules never caught on outside of the NAPBA, however, and were eventually forgotten.

The contest was one of the funniest performances ever witnessed and members and visitors went away loud in their praises of "Indoor Base Ball" as the new sport was christened.

GROWTH IN POPULARITY

Soon the game was being played throughout Chicago. The Farragut Boat Club team competed against other local squads. Indoor baseball, as it became known, gave athletes something to play in the winter months between the football and baseball seasons. By 1892 there were more than 100 club teams estimated to be playing in that Illinois city. Many of those early teams were for men, but reports suggest that women's teams existed as early as 1895.

▲ *A batter swings while a catcher and umpire look on during a 1919 softball game. Although the catcher is not wearing a glove, most players wore gloves at this time.*

Indoor baseball was a hit, but it wouldn't stay indoors for long. Hancock adapted his game to be played outside during the late 1800s. Soon variations of it began to spread to other cities across the nation.

One of those cities was Minneapolis, Minnesota. A fire department lieutenant named Lewis Rober Sr. was looking for a way to keep his firemen active and fit. So he organized an outdoor game in a vacant lot next to the firehouse. It was very similar to the game being played in Chicago.

Soon Rober was managing his own group of firefighters that called themselves the Kittens. The Kittens inspired the formation of other teams. By 1900, the competition in Minneapolis was being called Kitten League

Ball. Their games often attracted as many as 3,000 fans. Unlike baseball, it could be played quickly. Most games were completed in about 45 minutes. It was considered an ideal and safe after-dinner activity for men and women. Minneapolis boasted 64 men's teams and 25 women's teams by 1920. Today the city claims to be the birthplace of organized softball.

STANDARDIZING SOFTBALL

Minneapolis might claim to be the birthplace of organized softball, but that name did not even exist until 1926. That's when the term was first used in Denver, Colorado. In fact, the sport was known by various names during its early years. That is largely because the game's rules differed slightly depending on where it was played. That began to change during the 1920s and 1930s.

One of the first steps to standardize the rules for women's softball came in April 1923. That's when the Women's Division of the National Amateur Athletic Federation (NAAF) was founded. Under the sponsorship of the NAAF, a special set of rules was created for women.

Though the new game was called baseball for women, it most resembled modern fast-pitch softball. It featured smaller bats and a soft ball. The distances were shortened between bases, as well as from the pitching rubber to home plate.

A "FAIR" GAME

Chicago American sportswriter Leo Fischer and sporting goods salesman M. J. Pauley were leaders in bringing the various versions of softball together under one set of rules. One of their ideas was to bring several teams from around the nation together for a softball tournament. They had an ideal location. The 1933 World's Fair was taking place in Chicago. Fischer and Pauley decided to play the tournament at the Century of Progress Exposition at the fair.

A meeting was held beforehand to adopt standard rules for the sport and to give it a name. After all, it had

A Second Showcase

The 1933 World's Fair did not just mark a turning point for the sport of softball. It also provided a venue for what has become a highlight of the Major League Baseball season. The first All-Star Game was played in Chicago during the World's Fair. It was the brainchild of *Chicago Tribune* sports editor Arch Ward. The game pitted the greatest players from the American League against those from the National League. Nearly 48,000 fans showed up to Comiskey Park to watch the American League win. The All-Star Game has been played annually ever since. A celebrity softball game has become part of the weekend's festivities.

different rules and different names in different parts of the country. Only then did softball become the universally accepted name for the sport.

Fischer wrote story after story publicizing the event. He and Pauley drove around the country to invite championship softball teams to participate. They attracted 16 men's teams and eight women's teams from 16 states.

The tournament was a rousing success. More than 20 million people attended the World's Fair. Many of those who watched the softball event were surprised that women played the sport so well. An estimated 350,000 fans streamed in to witness the three-day tournament.

SLOWING IT DOWN

Softball was growing in popularity throughout the United States. As pitchers improved, however, it became increasingly harder for batters. So during the 1920s some local leagues changed the rules to require pitchers to put an arc on the ball. Slow-pitch softball had begun.

These floating pitches of slow-pitch softball were much easier for batters to hit. As such, this new style of play became popular. The 1933 World's Fair event was even divided into slow-pitch and fast-pitch tournaments.

As slow-pitch softball was easier for most people to play, it continued to grow in the United States. This was especially true among recreational players. However,

▲ *This woman watches the ball and runs to first base during a recreational softball game around 1943 in New York City.*

critics claimed that slow-pitch eliminated the need for pitchers who could get batters out by themselves. As such, fast-pitch softball remained the style of choice for top players.

▲ *Maye Noma catches while Tami Nagao bats during a 1942 game among members of the Chick-a-dee softball team.*

CHAPTER 3

A GROWING GAME

The popularity of softball was exploding during the years following the 1933 World's Fair. And much of the credit belonged to Leo Fischer and M. J. Pauley. They took the momentum the game built at the World's Fair and ran with it. In 1933, they founded the Amateur Softball Association of America (ASA), which brought structure to the sport. The group created state organizations and a set of rules to be followed across the country.

Fischer and Pauley's national tournament continued every year after the original 1933 event. A total of 88 men's and women's teams from the United States and Canada participated in 1937. The sport had grown so popular that two national radio networks broadcast some of the games.

Softball had proven to be cheap and quality entertainment. In 1938, *TIME* magazine proclaimed it to be "the spectator sport for folks with only a dime to spend."

By that time an estimated five million Americans were playing organized softball on 200,000 teams. In Los Angeles, California, alone there were 9,000 softball clubs, including 1,000 women's teams. A year later *Look* magazine claimed 11 million Americans had participated in the sport. Fischer even stated it had stolen the title of "national pastime" away from baseball.

During the early years of organized softball, more men played than women. However, the ASA reported in 1938 that more than one million women were playing softball. Fast-pitch softball did not become mostly a women's sport until the 1970s. That is when it began to flourish at the youth, high school, and college levels. But it was a popular game for females in many areas of the country well before then.

The Queen and Her Maids

Several great softball players used their talents to entertain fans. Among them was a pitcher from Texas named Rosie Beaird. She created a traveling softball team known as the Queen and Her Maids. Beginning with their first tour in 1965, the Queen and Her Maids traveled the country taking on local softball teams. They entertained crowds with their top-notch softball as well as their humorous antics. Among those who were part of the show was Rosie's brother, who wore a women's wig and used the nickname "Lotta Chatter." The team, which later changed its name to the Queen and Her Court, continued touring until 1990.

STARS OF THE SHOW

The women's game provided added entertainment through unusual uniforms. During the 1930s, many players wore shorts on the field, which differed from baseball players who wore pants. One championship team in New Mexico dressed in costumes inspired by the Native Americans of the Southwest. The Red Jackets of Wichita Falls, Texas, played barefoot and sung songs native to their state between innings.

By the 1940s, the Great Depression was over. However, the United States was embroiled in another problem: World War II. While millions of men were fighting overseas, a professional league was created for women to play a sport that was a mix of baseball and softball.

The All-American Girls Professional Baseball League (AAGPBL) boasted as many as 10 teams and gained great fame. It even inspired the hit 1992 movie titled *A League of Their Own*. The league featured a combination of baseball and softball. The size of the ball was larger than what was used in baseball. And pitchers were even allowed to throw the ball underhand, as is done in softball. The wartime league raided the rosters of the premier softball clubs to stock their teams.

The league operated from 1943 until 1954, hitting its peak in attendance in 1948. However, attendance dropped after that as World War II had finished in 1945 and many people's attention returned to baseball.

Women and Work

Some complained that the AAGPBL hurt the war effort during World War II. Many women worked in defense plants during that time. It was argued that allowing the players to travel for games kept them away from work. A rival league made a complaint to Major League Baseball commissioner Judge Kenesaw Mountain Landis. It was hoped Landis would disband the AAGPBL, which was run by a baseball owner and official. But Landis replied that Major League Baseball had no power to control the AAGPBL.

'Blazin' Bertha

A number of women made their marks in the 1950s and 1960s. But the first female softball star was "Blazin' Bertha" Tickey. She began pitching for the Alta Chevrolet team near her Dinuba, California, home at age 13. Tickey dominated the sport while playing for club teams around the United States. By the time she put away her glove 23 years later, she had recorded a career record of 762–88. Tickey pitched an incredible 161 **no-hitters**. She also helped set the stage for international women's softball competitions and pitched in the first World Championship tournament, which took place in Australia in 1965.

GOING GLOBAL

While women entertained crowds with softball in the United States during World War II, U.S. soldiers were introducing the sport to Europe and Asia. By 1952, the International Softball Federation (ISF) was founded. The ISF was created to govern amateur softball and international competition. Although the United States remained the dominant country in terms of participation and international results, the sport slowly but surely grew in countries such as Australia and Japan.

▲ Linda McConkey of the Lorelei Ladies softball team dives for third base during a 1955 game against the Atlanta Tomboys in Atlanta, Georgia.

▲ *Joan Joyce during her playing days with the Connecticut Falcons*

CHAPTER 4

BREAKING
THROUGH

In 1972, the U.S. Congress passed the Title IX legislation. It forced youth organizations, high schools, and colleges to provide equal funding for female and male athletics. New women's and girls' softball teams emerged in high schools and colleges throughout the country. Youth softball leagues for girls were also created. And though slow-pitch existed at those levels, fast-pitch was embraced by most. It proved far more exciting and challenging for the serious athletes.

Today, many girls play for a school softball team as well as an independent club team in the summer. The top high school players can play for college teams. There are three divisions within the National Collegiate Athletic Association (NCAA). Division I is the highest level. As softball has thrived in the United States, attempts have been made to establish professional leagues. However, those have proven harder to get started.

JOAN JOYCE

The International Women's Professional Softball League (IWPSL) was founded in 1976. Despite the name, all of the original teams were based throughout the United States. They played 120-game schedules. However, the league never enjoyed much mainstream popularity.

The premier player in the world did receive some recognition, though. Joan Joyce was nearing the end of her career when her team, the Raybestos Brakettes, became the Connecticut Falcons of the IWPSL. However, she was easily the new league's biggest star.

More than 6,500 fans watched her team play back-to-back **doubleheaders** in San Jose, California. Despite being 35 years old, Joyce sported a pitching record of 39–2 with an **earned-run average (ERA)** of just 0.13.

That translated into giving up an average of 0.13 runs per seven innings. And Joyce did not merely hit and pitch. She also served as the team owner and manager.

Many consider Joyce to be one of the greatest women's players in softball history. She threw an incredible 150 no-hitters during her 18-year career. She spent most of that time with the frequent ASA champion Brakettes, who were from Stratford, Connecticut. Women such as Joyce prompted some to hope that professional softball could and would flourish in the United States.

Dominating a Legend

How talented a pitcher was Joan Joyce? Boston Red Sox star Ted Williams, arguably the greatest hitter in baseball history, found out firsthand in August 1961. Joyce pitched to Williams in an exhibition game that year. Approximately 18,000 fans witnessed the event in Waterbury, Connecticut. Joyce threw 40 pitches to Williams, who made contact with his bat only twice. It was claimed that her fastball traveled over 100 miles per hour (161 km/h).

"She's a fantastic lady," said San Jose Sunbirds pitcher Charlotte Graham in 1976. "She's my idol. I've watched her closely for 10 years. She's truly the best player women's softball has ever had. I hope to see this professional

Many players today, such as this one, have returned to the traditional fast-pitch style of softball.

MODIFIED-PITCH

Modified-pitch softball is neither a slow-pitch nor fast-pitch game. The pitcher does not lob the ball. Nor can she use the traditional "windmill" windup that allows her to whip the ball with greater speed. She merely fires the ball as she steps forward.

The game was created in the 1960s as an alternative to fast-pitch, where the pitchers were almost too good. It copied slow-pitch in that it featured 10 players in the field. Modified-pitch took off with both men and women in various parts of the country. The new game was widely played during the 1970s. It was especially popular in Eastern states such as New York and Massachusetts, as well as Southern California. It later expanded into Michigan, Maryland, and Florida.

All the major softball organizations eventually added modified-pitch leagues. But the new style of play began losing participants and was slowly phased out. The ASA maintained its program. Some people still play modified-pitch, particularly in the Upper Midwest, but games are mostly recreational.

softball go over well enough for her to get the recognition she deserves."

It did not. An average of only 1,400 fans attended IWPSL games. Costs were too high. Income was too low. The players earned meager salaries of between $1,000 and $3,000 per season. The league folded after four short years. Joyce never received the appreciation given to equally talented athletes in other sports.

A BIG BOOST FOR THE SPORT

One significant move in 1982 gave younger softball players something to work toward. That is when the NCAA began hosting the College Softball World Series. It serves as the national championship round for Division I collegiate women's softball. The event, which is held in Oklahoma City, Oklahoma, has greatly helped increase visibility for the sport. Eight teams qualify for the College Softball World Series. They are divided into two groups, and the top team from each group meets in a best-of-three final series.

Many of the top women's softball players came from the Southwest United States. That was no surprise, as many top baseball players came from that area as well. The warm weather meant that players from that part of the country could practice their skills year-round. Teams from the Southwest have won 28 of 29 NCAA Division I championships through 2010. Division I schools are usually

▲ *A young shortstop prepares to throw out a runner at first base.*

the largest in the NCAA and have the best players. Those schools are able to offer scholarships to the top players to entice them there.

One program quickly rose above the rest, and that was the University of California, Los Angeles (UCLA). The UCLA Bruins won seven of the first 12 NCAA titles. They placed second three times. In winning three straight championships from 1988 to 1990, they compiled a remarkable 163–19 record.

The University of Arizona grew into the dominant force in Division I college softball during the 1990s. The Wildcats won five titles from 1991 to 1997. But the finest player of that era—and perhaps in the history of the sport—was UCLA pitcher Lisa Fernandez.

Fernandez was virtually unbeatable. During her four-year career with the Bruins, she compiled a record of 93–7. She owned a 0.22 career ERA. That translated into giving up an average of 0.22 runs per seven innings. Fernandez sported the lowest ERA in college softball in both 1992 (0.14) and 1993 (0.25). She led the Bruins to a 54–2 mark and an NCAA championship in 1992 with her 29–0 record. She even pitched two no-hitters in the 1993 College World Series.

Fernandez was also a fine hitter who improved with age. She led all of college softball with a .510 batting average as a senior. She ranks among the best hitters ever at UCLA. Asked in 1995 about the reason for her success, Fernandez gave a simple answer.

"Instead of a 'secret' movement or some extra flick, my answer is practice," she said. "Hours and hours of practice, day after day, week after week. It's not simple, and it's not easy, but it works—as long as you do it often and work hard.

"But you have to remember. Practice does not make perfect. It's the right kind of practice that makes perfect.

▲ *UCLA star Lisa Fernandez prepares to hurl a pitch during one of her college games.*

And even then it's tough. I've been playing fast-pitch soft-ball since I was eight years old, and I still have days that nothing goes right."

Opposing players might have been surprised to hear that. They were relieved when she graduated from UCLA, but she was just beginning to make her mark. The decision to make softball part of the Olympic Games in 1996 placed it on the biggest international stage. And Fernandez would play a huge role in making the United States the best team in the world.

▲ Japan's Emi Tsukada (8) rounds the bases for a home run as her manager looks on during the 1996 Olympic Games.

CHAPTER 5

GOING GLOBAL

Softball was invented in the United States and has long enjoyed more popularity there than in other countries. However, since U.S. servicemen began spreading the game overseas in the 1940s, the game has continued to grow internationally. By 1965, the game had grown enough for the ISF to justify creating the Women's World

Championship. That tournament, which at the time was held approximately every four years, pits the world's top national teams against each other. National teams are made up of the top players from each country. However, in the early years the United States instead sent the ASA champion.

The first World Championship took place in 1965 in Australia. Five teams took part in that tournament. They were Australia, Japan, New Guinea, New Zealand, and the United States. Australia won the gold medal while Team USA took the silver medal. Japan finished third. Japan won the gold medal on home soil at the next World Championship, in 1970. The United States again took second place.

World Tour

There was enough global interest to hold the first World Championship in 1965, but softball was very much a growing sport outside of the United States. One of the top teams in the United States at the time was the Raybestos Brakettes from Stratford, Connecticut. In fact, the team was the ASA champion that year and represented the United States at the World Championship. After winning a silver medal there, the Brakettes went on a world tour to promote softball. They traveled to 10 countries in 37 days working with players and coaches to help advance the sport worldwide.

U.S. DOMINANCE

Following the 1970 World Championship, it became a rare occurrence for the U.S. team to finish anything but first in international competitions. Between 1974 and 2010, the World Championship was held 10 times. Team USA won all but one of those tournaments, when New Zealand took the title in 1982. The U.S. team's margin of victory during nearly every event was astounding. It went undefeated in winning its first five championships. In those years, the team outscored its opponents, 324–13.

In 1974 Team USA was arguably better than any team in the history of international sport. The Americans outscored their competition, 75–0, in the World Championship that year. The hero was pitcher Joan Joyce, who averaged more than two strikeouts an inning. She pitched three no-hitters and two **perfect games** in the event.

In 1990, the United States began sending an all-star team to the World Championship rather than the ASA champion. The popularity of youth and college softball in the United States helped Team USA remain a step ahead of its international opponents, where softball is not as popular. However, other countries such as Australia, Canada, Japan, and New Zealand have continued to improve.

A BIG BOOST

By 1991, seven Women's World Championship tournaments had taken place. Six different countries had hosted the event, including the United States twice. At the time, the International Olympic Committee (IOC) was looking to add women's sports to the Olympic Games. With softball growth around the world, the IOC decided the sport would be a good fit. So softball made its Olympic debut at the 1996 Games in Atlanta, Georgia.

The United States was heavily favored to win the gold medal on home soil. From 1986 until the beginning of the 1996 Games, Team USA had gone 110–1 in international competition. In 1994, the U.S. team went undefeated in 10 games to win the World Championship. Eight of the wins were shutouts.

By 1996, though, other countries were making strides. Team USA found that out the hard way. After easily winning its first five Olympic games, the U.S. squad played Australia in a first-round game. The teams held each other scoreless through nine innings. Then Team USA took a 1–0 lead in the top of the tenth. With U.S. pitcher Lisa Fernandez throwing a no-hitter to that point, a U.S. win appeared inevitable.

Nobody told Joanne Brown that. The Australian batter stepped to the plate with two outs and one runner on base in the bottom of the tenth. With one strike remaining, Brown connected on a pitch and sent it over the fence for a two-run home run. Australia had handed Team USA only its second loss since 1986. However, Team USA

▲ *Australian players celebrate Joanne Brown's two-run homer that gave their team a victory over Team USA at the 1996 Olympic Games.*

still moved on to the second round due to its record in the other first-round games.

Team USA also faced tough competition from China during the 1996 Games. Although Team USA beat China in first-round play and also the semifinals, both wins were only by one run. The two squads met again in the gold-medal game. Team USA again won, this time 3–1. However, the Chinese team argued that a two-run homer by U.S. star Dot Richardson should have been called a foul.

Despite the controversial ending, the first Olympic softball tournament was considered a rousing success.

The following excerpt from a *Sports Illustrated* article described the impact softball made on the event that year:

> *Women's softball . . . took these Olympics by storm. [Ticket sellers] were getting $300 a seat for the gold medal softball game between the U.S. and China in 8,500-seat Golden Park, and throughout the tournament the U.S. games were sellouts.*

SHINING STARS

If one factor defined Team USA's run to the 1996 gold medal, it was dominant pitching. Fernandez and Michele Granger led a pitching staff that surrendered just six runs throughout the tournament. However, in the following

Tanya Harding

The strong U.S. pitchers often dominated the news as they led Team USA to three straight Olympic gold medals from 1996 to 2004. But Australian pitcher Tanya Harding also displayed her vast talents at the Olympic level. In four Olympic Games from 1996 to 2008, she gave up just 13 total runs in 109 innings pitched. She pitched a 10-inning shutout against Team USA in 1996. But she saved her best for her home fans in 2000. That is when she struck out 18 U.S. batters during 13 innings of work in Australia's 2–1 victory over Team USA. It was among the best performances in Olympic history.

years, pitchers from around the world were improving as well.

The gap between Team USA and the other teams appeared to be closing even more at the 2000 Olympic Games in Sydney, Australia. There, for the first time in history, the U.S. squad lost three straight games. They were a 2–1 loss to Japan, a 2–0 loss to China in 14 innings, and a 2–1 loss to Australia in 13 innings. However, Team USA was still alive in the tournament. In fact, it recovered to reach the gold-medal game. In that game, Team USA needed extra innings to defeat Japan 2–1 and win its second gold medal. Australia took the bronze medal for the second time.

A DOMINANT PERFORMANCE

The ISF felt the pitching—particularly that of Team USA—was simply getting too strong. So it ruled that the mound would be pushed back from 40 feet (12.2 m) to 43 feet (13.1 m) from home plate for the 2004 Olympic Games in Athens, Greece. That would reduce the speed of pitches. It would also force pitchers to rely on movement of their pitches.

At the 2004 Games, however, the U.S. pitching staff was as dominant as ever. The pitchers kept batters off-balance by changing speeds on the ball. They also threw to different locations within the strike zone.

The U.S. quartet of Fernandez, Lori Harrigan, a young Cat Osterman, and Jennie Finch hurled shutout after shutout. Team USA gave up just one run the entire tournament—and that was in the championship game. Team USA defeated Australia 5–1 to claim its third straight Olympic gold medal. Japan finished with the bronze medal.

"This team is the best I have ever been associated with," U.S. coach Mike Candrea said. "They are a special group that will go down in history as the most dominant team to ever take the field. All of the countless hours spent in the weight room and on the practice field finally paid off for this exceptional group of athletes."

Jennie Finch helped attract new fans who otherwise might not have watched softball.

NOT MANY LIKE JENNIE

Jennie Finch combined talent, personality, and beauty to become a star. She was one of the premier pitchers in the history of college softball. She set an NCAA record by winning 60 games without a loss at the University of Arizona. She also starred for Team USA at the 2004 and 2008 Olympic Games. Her achievements, looks, and fun persona landed her many TV appearances. She could also be seen in magazines such as Glamour and Vanity Fair. Finch's ability to identify with people who did not follow the sport helped it grow.

▲ *Pitcher Yukiko Ueno (center) and Japan celebrate a bittersweet gold medal at the 2008 Olympic Games.*

CHAPTER 6

PLAYING TO WIN

Softball had only appeared in three Olympic Games in 2005. However, the IOC voted to eliminate the sport from the Olympic program starting in 2012. A petition to have it reinstated for the 2016 Games was later rejected. Some believe the IOC made the move because Team USA had dominated the event.

A SURPRISE ENDING

The world's best softball players still had one more opportunity to compete at the Olympic Games in 2008 when they were held in Beijing, China. As it had been in the three previous editions, Team USA entered the competition as favorites to win another gold medal. The U.S. players backed it up early by winning their first eight games by a combined score of 57–2.

Two of those victories were achieved against Japan. The Asian nation had established itself as one of the top softball nations in the world at that point. However, when Team USA and Japan met again in the gold-medal game, many assumed the U.S. team would again defeat Japan and march to its fourth straight Olympic gold medal.

That was not the case. With U.S. star Cat Osterman pitching, Japan took a 2–0 lead after 3 1/2 innings. Team USA closed the gap when third baseman Crystl Bustos hit a solo home run in the bottom of the fourth. But that was its only run.

Japan's **ace** Yukiko Ueno pitched a complete game, keeping Team USA off the scoreboard after that. Meanwhile, Japan added another run in the seventh inning. The final score: Japan 3, Team USA 1.

Washington Post reporter Dave Sheinin described the scene as the Japanese and U.S. athletes waited to receive their medals.

"The Japanese champions [were] literally quaking with glee and the stunned Americans [were] scarcely trying to hide their disappointment," he wrote. "The television cameraman lingered on the famous face of pitcher Jennie Finch, whose cheeks were lined with tears. Osterman waved and flashed a grim-faced glance to her family in the stands."

After three Olympic Games in which Team USA had dominated, Japan finally broke through and won the gold medal. Emerging countries such as Japan and Australia would have more opportunities to go for gold medals—but it would have to be in the World Championship. Although the ISF is working hard to get the sport back into the Olympic Games, the star players of 2008 would likely be too old to still be competing if it ever gets back in.

"It hurts a lot," Bustos said. "You train your whole life and you want to win. We're competitors. . . . You don't want it to end this way."

NEW BEGINNINGS

Softball might no longer be in the Olympic Games, but it is still thriving at the youth, high school, college, professional, and even the international level. The Women's World Championship is now held every two years. In addition, new competitions such as the World Cup of Softball give top national teams an opportunity to compete against each other. The ASA has hosted various national teams at

▲ *Team USA's Jessica Mendoza steps on home plate to score a run against Japan during the 2010 Women's World Championship.*

the World Cup of Softball in all non-Olympic years since 2005.

U.S. outfielder Jessica Mendoza expects to be starring in those competitions for years to come. Mendoza had been one of the finest college players ever. She was a three-time Athlete of the Year at Stanford University in the NCAA's Division I. She then embarked on a brilliant career with the U.S. national team.

In the 60-game tour leading up to the 2008 Olympic Games, Mendoza led the team with a .495 batting average, 25 doubles, and 107 runs batted in. She also slugged two home runs in the playoffs to lead the Florida Pride to the National Pro Fastpitch (NPF) title in 2010.

INTERNATIONAL STARS

The United States has traditionally dominated the international softball scene. The world is quickly catching up, though. Pitcher Tanya Harding was one of the first international stars of the Olympic era. She led Australia to four Olympic medals in the four Olympic competitions. Other players have followed in her footsteps.

NPF

No women's professional fast-pitch league has enjoyed great success. The NPF hopes to change that. The league began playing in 2004. The Chicago Bandits made a splash that December by signing star pitcher Jennie Finch to a contract. Olympic star and slugger Crystl Bustos joined the Akron Racers. In 2007, pitcher Cat Osterman began competing for the Rockford Thunder. But the NPF has struggled to find stability. Franchises were born and quickly died. Attendance at games was low. Only four teams were still in the league in 2010. However, the league remained alive, giving young softball players a goal to strive for.

Monica Abbott

Pitcher Monica Abbott set a number of NCAA records at the University of Tennessee. Abbott fired an incredible 23 no-hitters and six perfect games during her college career. She was named USA Softball College Player of the Year in 2007. She also enjoyed an amazing run in international competition. Abbott did not surrender any runs in the Pan American Games or World Championship in 2006 and 2007. The Pan American Games are a multisport competition between athletes from North, Central, and South America.

Yukiko Ueno turned many heads with her performance at the 2008 Olympic Games. The Japanese hurler held Team USA to just one run in seven innings in the gold-medal game. That was far from her first feat, though. At the 2004 Games, Ueno threw the first perfect game in Olympic history as Japan beat China 2–0. She is known as one of the hardest-throwing pitchers in softball.

Another Japanese star, center fielder Eri Yamada, also starred in that 2008 gold-medal game. She batted 2-for-3 and hit a solo home run in the win.

Pitcher Danielle Lawrie was supposed to be a junior at the University of Washington in 2008. Instead, she joined the Canadian national team at the Olympic Games. The 21-year-old pitched in three games, helping Canada finish fourth. Then she returned to Washington and finished off an amazing college career. As a junior in 2009, Lawrie led the Huskies to their first-ever NCAA Division 1 title. She was named the collegiate player of the year in both 2009 and 2010 before joining the Florida Pride in NPF.

The Olympic dream is over for now. But the sport of softball is still very much alive—especially in the United States. Youth and high school softball remain some of the most popular girls' sports in the country. Meanwhile, the College Softball World Series has developed into one of the highest-profile collegiate women's championships. And with the NPF and international play to strive for, there are still plenty of major competitions to dream of winning.

▲ UCLA players await teammate Andrea Harrison at home plate after Harrison hit a grand slam during the 2010 College Softball World Series.

GLOSSARY

ace: A team's top pitcher.

at-bat: A plate appearance by an individual batter. It can result in a hit, a walk, or an out.

balls: Pitches deemed by an umpire to be out of the hitting zone. Four balls constitute a walk, which allows the batter to take first base.

diamond: Another name for a softball field; given its name for the shape of the infield.

doubleheaders: Back-to-back games played on the same day.

earned run average (ERA): A measurement of a pitcher's effectiveness that calculates runs given up per inning pitched.

extra innings: If a game is tied after seven innings, extra innings are added one at a time until one team wins.

force: A play in which a base runner must advance, therefore allowing the defense to record an out simply by gaining possession of the ball and touching the base that the runner is approaching.

foul: A ball that is hit outside the field of play.

hit: A ball hit by a batter and not caught by a fielder, therefore allowing the batter to reach base.

home plate: The fourth base and the one that gives a team a run scored when reached by a runner.

home run: A ball hit that travels over the fence or a hit in which a batter reaches all three bases and home plate.

innings: Segments of a softball game in which both teams have recorded three outs. Each game has seven.

no-hitters: Games in which a pitcher allows no hits.

perfect games: Games in which the pitcher does not allow any batters to reach a base.

pitching rubber: The slab a pitcher must be touching with one or both feet when she pitches.

professional: An athlete or any person who gets paid for her work.

rally: A combination of hits and walks that results in a run, or runs, being scored.

runs: Scores given to a team when a runner has reached all three bases and home plate.

shutout: A game or inning in which one team doesn't score.

steal: Once the pitcher lets go of the ball, a base runner in fast-pitch softball can try to advance to the next base.

strike: A pitch deemed by an umpire to be in the hitting zone.

strike zone: An invisible area directly above home plate. If a ball passes through the strike zone, it is considered a strike.

umpire: The person responsible for calling balls and strikes or determining whether a runner is safe or out in a game.

walk: If a pitcher throws four balls in one at-bat, the batter automatically takes first base.

FOR MORE
INFORMATION

BOOKS

Finch, Jennie. *Throw Like a Girl*. Chicago: Triumph Books, 2011.
This is a story of success about Jennie Finch and her many
brilliant pitching performances.

Kempf, Cheri. *The Softball Pitching Edge*. Champaign, IL:
Human Kinetics, 2002.
This book teaches readers how to gain advantages over hitters.

Noren, Rick. *Softball Fundamentals: A Better Way to Learn the
Basics*. Champaign, IL: Human Kinetics, 2005.
Learn how to do everything better on a softball field through
this book.

Sammons, Barry. *Fastpitch Softball: The Windmill Pitcher*. New
York: McGraw-Hill, 1997.
This book explains how to make the most out of your talent as
a fast-pitch pitcher.

Smith, Dick. *Fast Pitch Softball Fundamentals*. Terre Haute, IN:
Wish Publishing, 2004.
One of the top coaches in the sport teaches the basics of
softball.

WEBSITES

All Star Activities: Softball Positions
www.allstaractivities.com/sports/softball/softball-positions.htm
Learn about the responsibilities of each position on the softball field.

Cat Osterman
www.catosterman.com
The official website of Cat Osterman features a biography, photos, videos, and news about the U.S. Olympic gold-medal pitcher.

Fastpitch.us
www.fastpitch.us/joan-joyce-the-missing-legend-ted-williams-could-not-touch
The story of pitcher Joan Joyce and her amazing performance against baseball great Ted Williams is recounted here.

NCAA Division I Softball
www.ncaa.com/sports/softball/d1
The schedules, ranking, statistics, and history of the biggest and best college softball teams in the nation can be found on this website.

USA Softball
www.usasoftball.com/folders.asp?uid=1
Learn all about the U.S. women's softball team here, including upcoming events, videos, and information about top college programs.

INDEX

Abbott, Monica, 55
Akron Racers, 54
All-American Girls
   Professional Baseball
   League (AAGPBL), 31
Alta Chevrolet, 32
Amateur Softball Association
   of America (ASA), 28, 29,
   36, 37, 43, 44, 52
Australia, 32, 43, 44, 45, 46,
   47, 48, 49, 52, 54

baseball, 5, 7, 18, 21, 22, 23,
   24, 25, 29, 30, 31, 36, 38
batter, 6, 7, 8, 9, 10, 12, 13,
   15, 16, 17, 18, 23, 26, 27,
   45, 48
batting order, 6, 7, 17–18, 40,
   54
Beaird, Rosie, 30
Brown, Joanne, 45, 46
Bustos, Crystl, 51, 52, 54

Canada, 44, 55
Candrea, Mike, 49
catching, 8, 9, 15
Chicago Bandits, 54
China, 46, 47, 48, 51, 55
College Softball World Series,
   38, 40, 56
Connecticut Falcons, 35, 36,
   43

equipment, 18

Farragut Boat Club, 20, 22
Fernandez, Lisa, 40–44, 45,
   47, 49
Finch, Jennie, 49, 52, 54
Fischer, Leo, 25, 26, 28, 29
Florida Pride, 54, 56

Graham, Charlotte, 36
Granger, Michelle, 47
Great Depression, 30

Hancock, George, 21, 23
Harding, Tanya, 47, 54
Harrigan, Lori, 49

Indoor Base Ball Guide, 21
International Olympic
   Committee (IOC), 45, 50
International Softball
   Federation (ISF), 32, 42,
   48, 52
International Women's
   Professional Softball
   League (IWPSL), 35, 38

Japan, 32, 43, 44, 48, 49, 51,
   52, 55
Joyce, Joan, 35, 36, 38, 44

Kitten League Ball, 23–24

Landis, Judge Kenesaw Mountain, 31
Lawrie, Danielle, 55, 56

Major League Baseball, 25, 31
Mendoza, Jessica, 53, 54
modified-pitch, 37

National Collegiate Athletic Association (NCAA), 35, 38, 39, 40, 49, 53, 55, 56
National Pro Fastpitch (NPF), 5, 55, 56
New Zealand, 43, 44

Olympic Games
    1996, 41, 45, 46, 47
    2000, 48
    2004, 4, 48, 49, 55
    2008, 4, 49, 51, 54, 55
Osterman, Cat, 4, 5, 49, 51, 52, 54

Pan American Games, 55
Pauley, M. J., 25, 26, 28, 29
positions, 7, 12–13, 15, 17

Queen and Her Maids, the, 30

Raybestos Brakettes, 35, 36, 43
Richardson, Dot, 46
Rober Sr., Lewis, 23

Rockford Thunder, 54

San Jose Sunbirds, 36
Sheinin, Dave, 51
slow-pitch, 4, 5, 18–19, 26, 27, 34, 37
Smith, Dick "Smitty," 16

Team USA, 4, 43, 44, 45, 46, 47, 48, 49, 50, 51, 52, 55
Tickey, "Blazin' Bertha," 32
Title IX, 34

Ueno, Yukiko, 51, 55
umpire, 8, 23, 27, 29

Ward, Arch, 25
Williams, Ted, 36
Women's Division of the National Amateur Athletic Federation (NAAF), 24
Women's World Championship, 32, 42–45, 52, 55
    1965, 32, 43
    1970, 43
    1974, 44
    1990, 44
    1994, 45
World's Fair, 25–26, 28

Yamada, Eri, 55

PLACES TO VISIT

National Softball Hall of Fame and Museum

2801 NE 50th Street, Oklahoma City, OK 73111
(405) 424-5266
www.asasoftball.com/hall_of_fame/index.asp
This hall of fame and museum features information and
exhibits about the most important players and other people
in the history of softball. It is part of the ASA Hall of Fame
Complex, which has some of the finest softball facilities in
the world and also plays host to several major softball events
each year, such as U.S. national team games and the Women's
College World Series.

ABOUT THE AUTHOR

Marty Gitlin is a freelance writer based in
Cleveland, Ohio. He has written more than 40
educational books. Gitlin has won more than 45
awards during his 25 years as a writer, including
First Place for General Excellence from the
Associated Press. He lives with his wife and
three children.

ABOUT THE CONTENT CONSULTANT

After a long history with the ASA of America
and USA Softball programs as a National Team
player, a two-time world champion, and a Pan
American Games Champion, Karen (Sanchelli)
Johns joined the USA Softball Women's National
Team coaching staff in 2005. She most notably
served as an assistant with the 2008 Women's
National Team, which won a silver medal at the 2008 Olympic
Games, and as the head coach of the 2010–11 Junior Women's
National Team. She and her husband have one daughter. The
family resides in Trussville, Alabama.